This book belongs to:

_____

_____

_____

Thank you to Bob for 'one tiny dot' of an idea.
LR

To Max, the kindest boy I know, lots of love Mum x
GM

A TEMPLAR BOOK

First published in the UK in 2022 by Templar Books,
an imprint of Bonnier Books UK
4th Floor, Victoria House,
Bloomsbury Square, London WC1B 4DA
Owned by Bonnier Books
Sveavägen 56, Stockholm, Sweden
www.bonnierbooks.co.uk

Text copyright © 2022 by Lucy Rowland
Illustration copyright © 2022 by Gwen Millward
Design copyright © 2022 by Templar Books

3 5 7 9 10 8 6 4 2

ISBN 978-1-78741-886-8

This book was typeset in Mr Lucky and Mr Dodo
The illustrations were created with
pen, ink, crayon, pencil and coloured digitally

Edited by Alison Ritchie
Designed by Adam Allori
Production by Neil Randles

Printed in China

MIX
Paper from
responsible sources
FSC® C104723

templar
books

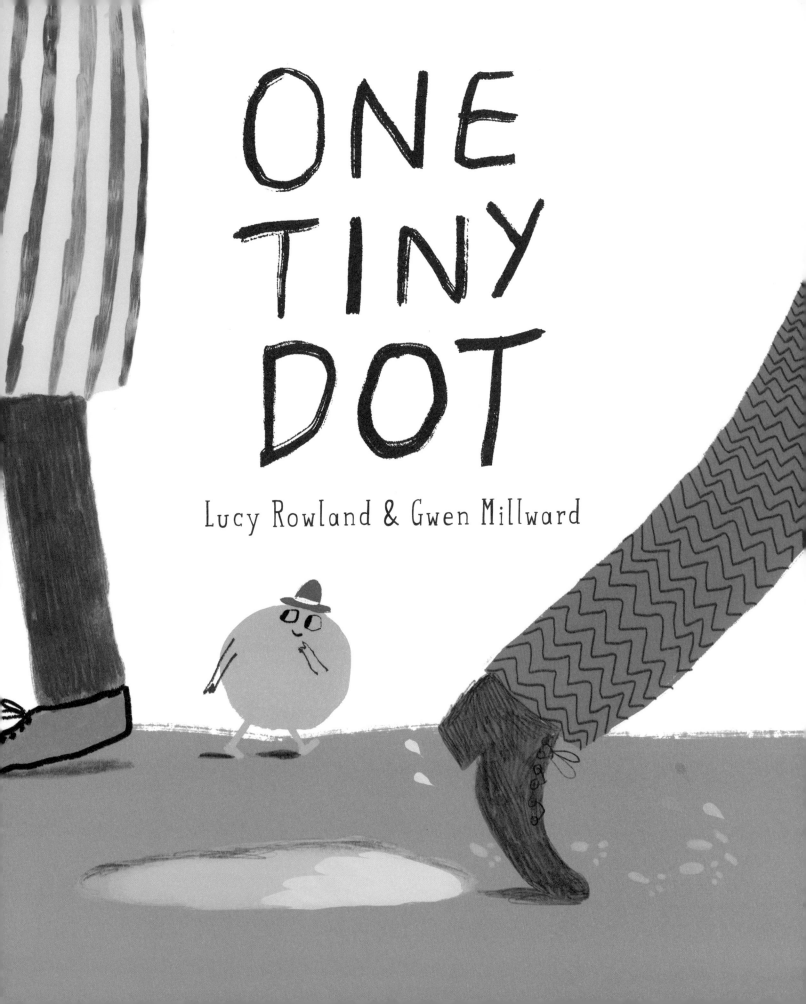

# ONE TINY DOT

Lucy Rowland & Gwen Millward

There once was a dot, who was really quite small,
walking along and not minding at all
that it wasn't that big or that bold or that tough,

for this dot was **KINDNESS**
and that was enough.

Along came a boy
wearing trainers brand new.
And KINDNESS thought
**they're nice!**
and jumped on his shoe.

"**Hi!**" said the boy
and he gave a big smile,
then added,
"**You're welcome to
stay for a while.**"

That's nice!
thought the dot
and it grew a bit **BIGGER**.

(The boy had been **KIND** you see
– that was the trigger.)

For now that small dot
was more like a dash –
and it felt very happy
till suddenly . . .

# "MY SHOES ARE SOAKED THROUGH!"

cried the boy with a howl.
But along came a girl who said,

**"Borrow my towel!"**

*"How kind!"* said the boy
and the dot grew quite **TALL**
and then it grew **WIDER** – the size of a ball!

So they rolled along happily
– boy, dot and girl –
till they met a small
gathering, all in a whirl.

A little old gentleman
turned to the three,
and he told them,
**"My kitten is stuck
up that tree!"**

"**We'll help you,**" they said (for the man looked so sad). The man was relieved, and the dot felt so glad.

The others helped too, so the dot became gladder and grew once again to the size of a ladder.

They walked through the fields.
The dot led the way.
Behind them flowed KINDNESS,
throughout the whole day.

The smiles, the thank-yous,
the crowds – they all grew.

And that small dot of KINDNESS?

# It kept growing too!

When they got to the town, it filled up
**a WHOLE lot**
with the KINDNESS that came
from that very small dot.

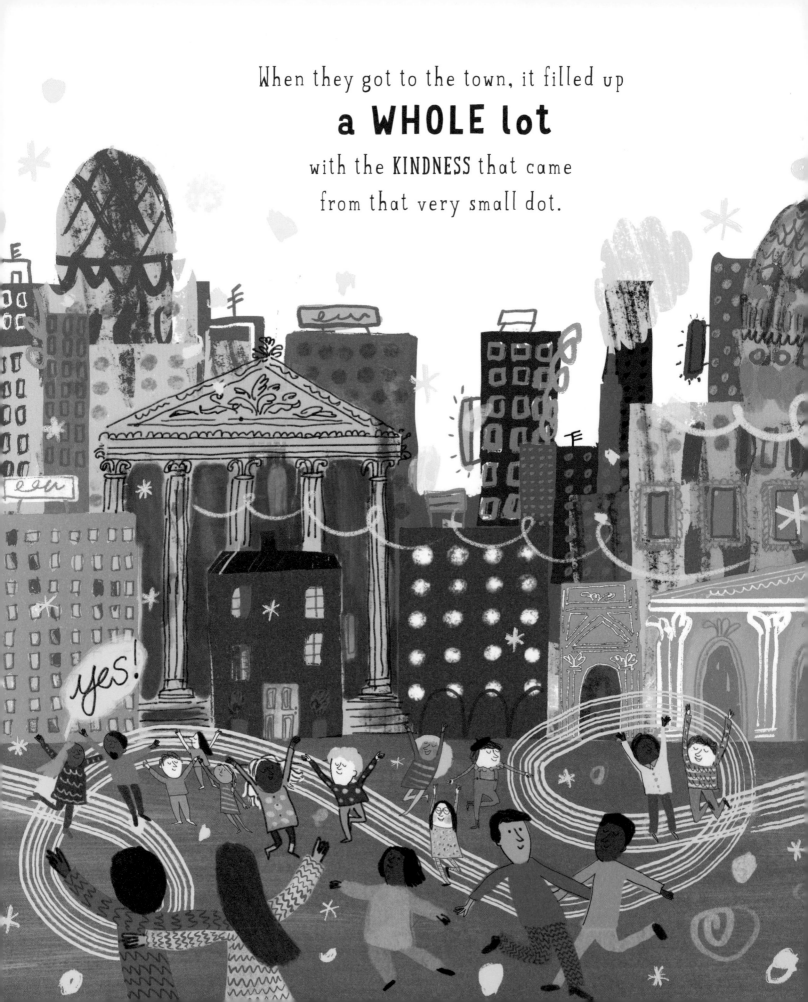

See the thing is with KINDNESS
– it spreads if you let it.
Just pass on a **smile** and
you'll never regret it.

The mayor of the town said,
"Let's head to the sea!
**You've all been so kind!**
The ice creams are on me."

So they swept right along
behind **KINDNESS** until
they came to a stop
at the top of a hill.

There stood a girl
and an **ANGER** as well,
not small like a dot
**BUT BIG LIKE A YELL!**

Large like a thundercloud
**RUMBLING** around.
The girl clenched her fists
as she **STAMPED** on the ground.

The **ANGER** grew **BIGGER**
and turned into fire,
with flickering flames
reaching **HIGHER**
and **HIGHER**.

This ANGER was
# BIG.
It was
# BOLD,
it was
# TOUGH.

It must be put out . . .
but was KINDNESS enough?

Well . . . the thing is with Anger
(as KINDNESS well knew),
if you look really hard,
you'll see SADNESS there too.

So **KINDNESS** helped **SADNESS**
to hold its head high . . .

# "PLEASE come to our PARTY!"

it said with a cry.

The roars became *whispers*,
the **thunder** grew still.

With arms in the air,
they all flew down the hill.

Right to the bottom and
straight to the sea.

They ran through the sand
and felt pleased as could be!

The mayor was pleased too,
and he started to beam . . .

as he handed out thank-yous
and strawberry ice cream.

Then the whole of the town
had a **PARTY** that night.

They watched the sun set
and they danced in its light.

When they headed for
home, they left not a jot.

Except for their
footprints . . .

. . . and one tiny dot.